The Big Boasting Battle

THIS BOOK WAS DONATED BY Laura Michela

1996

ISBN 0-590-22211-2

Copyright © 1995 by Hans Wilhelm, Inc.
All rights reserved. Published by Scholastic Inc.

12 11 10 9 8 7 6 5 4 3 2 1   5 6 7 8 9/9 0/0

Printed in the U.S.A.   14

First Scholastic printing, April 1995

The Big Boasting Battle

by HANS WILHELM

SCHOLASTIC INC.

New York Toronto London Auckland Sydney

It was four o'clock in the afternoon.
Sylvester was late again.

Horace, the lion, was getting impatient.
He couldn't wait to tell his friend about all
the things he had seen and done, or was
going to see and do.

It was no fun having tea and cookies
alone with no one to impress.

Suddenly Horace heard Sylvester slithering
through the grass.

"You are late!" said Horace.

"Maybe," said Sylvester, "but I don't know why I should always have to come to your place. *You* should come to visit *me*."

"Don't make me laugh!" Horace said. "You forget who I am. A lion is the king of the animals."

"Pooh. What's so great about that?" Sylvester wanted to know. "We snakes were around long before you guys were even born."

"That's ancient history!" Horace scoffed.
"Strength is what counts. And no one is
stronger than a lion!"

"Maybe so," said Sylvester, "but you forget
that snakes are stupendously more intelligent
than lions!"

"Oh, yeah?" said Horace. "Well, a lion can roar louder than any other animal." And he gave a frightful roar.

Sylvester was still not impressed. "But I can swim faster than you!" He zipped across the river and was up on the bank again in a flash.

"Also," Sylvester continued, "I'm better at hiding!"

"So what?" Horace said. "You can't dance as wild as I can!"

"And," he continued, "you can't climb a tree and look out over the whole forest!"

"Big deal," Sylvester said. "I can hide in the smallest hole — but you can't."

"I'm
a
mile
taller
than
you!"
Horace said.

"And I'm a mile longer than you!" Sylvester said.

"I bet you can't
hold your breath
as long as I can,"
Horace said.

"And I bet you can't stand
on your head as straight as I can!"
Sylvester boasted.

"I have a beautiful fuzzy mane,"
Horace boasted back.
"And you don't!"

"Who wants to look like a dust mop?"
replied Sylvester.

"Besides, I'm more acrobatic than you!"

"That's not true," Horace said, "because I
can jump higher than you can!"

"But I can run faster than you!" Sylvester said.

"No, you can't!"

"Yes, I can!"

"No, you can't!"

"Yes, I can!"

"Nonsense!" Horace yelled finally. "Snakes don't run as fast as lions!"

"You're right, they don't," Sylvester said. "They run even *faster*."

Now Horace's blood was really boiling. "Let's see who runs faster. I dare you to race me!"

"You're on!" Sylvester cried.

"Okay," said Horace. "I'll count to three. Ready? One . . . two . . . three . . . GO!"

And off they went. Across the plain, over
the ditches, around the trees, and through
the tall grass...

...until the ground suddenly gave in.
Through dried leaves and branches they fell
into a deep hole!

Down, down they fell until they landed
with a thud on the bottom.

"Holy Hippopotamus!" moaned Horace. "What is this?"

"I think we have fallen into a trap," Sylvester said.

"A *trap*? Oh, no! We have to get out. Quick!"

"There is no way out of here," said Sylvester in a gloomy voice. "The sides are too high. And unless you can grow wings, we've had it!"

"But I don't want to get caught," cried Horace, "and be locked up in a circus cage."

"Neither do I," said Sylvester, "but there's nothing we can do."

"Wait. Don't give up so easily. Think a little! Didn't you say snakes are smarter than lions?"

"That's true, but the fact that lions are stronger doesn't help us, either."

Horace started to pace in circles. "Naturally we cannot expect any help from the zebras or the giraffes. They are probably already celebrating because the lion has fallen into a trap."

"Why don't you sit down?" Sylvester was getting nervous. "You're going to stomp on my tail. There's hardly enough room here to swing a cat — if you'll pardon the expression."

Horace looked up at the branch above the trap. "Swing a cat?" he said. Then he laughed. "That's IT! What a brilliant idea!"

"Maybe there's not enough room to swing a cat...but there is just enough room to swing a snake," Horace cheered. "Hold on!" Then he grabbed Sylvester's tail and whirled him round and round...

. . .and tossed him up toward the tree branch.
The clever snake quickly tied himself
into a knot around the branch. Now Horace
had a perfect "rope" to climb out of the
trap.

The two friends were overjoyed when they
realized that they were free again!

"I hate to admit it," Sylvester said, "but I'm very happy that lions are so strong."

"And I'm happy that snakes are so smart," Horace replied. "After all, it was your idea that saved us."

"But without your strength, I never would have reached that tree branch," Sylvester admitted.

"I guess we are both perfect in our different ways," Horace said. "And I am mighty grateful for that!"

From then on, Horace and Sylvester did not argue about where they would meet for tea and cookies. Every afternoon they got together under the old baobab tree, which was exactly halfway between their two homes.

And they were always on time.